Early one summer morning the postman rang the bell. Benny nearly fell down the stairs in his hurry to open the door.

"Is it for me?" he cried, seeing a great big parcel.

But it wasn't for Benny. The parcel was a birthday present for his big brother, Tom.

Benny and his little sister Becky helped Tom tear off the brown paper. Dad was so busy watching them that he nearly burnt the bacon.

The parcel was full of orange-coloured material.

"Whatever is it?" said Benny.

"It's a tent!" cried Tom excitedly. "It's from Uncle Roger. A real camping tent!"

"Aren't you lucky," sighed Benny. "I've always wanted a tent."

As they ate their breakfast Dad asked Tom if he wanted a birthday party.

Tom frowned. "I'm too big for a party this year," he said.

Tom was going to be twelve on Saturday.

"Oh! But you must have a party!" cried Becky. "It won't be a proper birthday without a party!"

Then Dad had an idea.

"Maybe you could have a small camping party, Tom. You could pitch the tent in the garden, have a special tea and camp outside for the night."

Tom brightened up. "Yes! I could ask Sam and Max," he said, helping himself to more toast.

That night Tom got out his special notebook and began to write busily.

"What are you doing?" said Benny, coming to sit on the end of Tom's bed.

"I'm making a list of all the things I'll need for the camp," said Tom importantly. "Things like sausages and a really good torch . . ."

"Camping sounds such good fun. Are you really going to cook outside? Please could I come to your tent party?" said Benny.

"You're too young," said Tom. "You wouldn't enjoy it."

"PLEASE let me!" said Benny.

"Oh, all right," Tom smiled. "But I'll have to ask Dad."

Benny bounced up and down on Tom's bed in excitement.

Dad was not sure about the new plan at first.

"Benny's too small to camp out all night," he said.

"I'll look after him, Dad," said Tom, putting his arm round Benny. "He'll be all right, honestly!"

And so it was settled. Tom, his two friends Sam and Max, *and* his little brother Benny would camp out on Saturday night. Benny could hardly wait.

On Saturday morning Benny helped Tom with the shopping for the camp. They bought sausages and baked beans. They bought fizzy drinks and a good torch.

In the afternoon Sam and Max came round. They got out the new orange tent. They pitched it at the very end of the garden, behind the blackberry bushes. Benny hammered in the tent pegs with a big wooden mallet.

Sam had brought a little camping stove. Benny rushed to see it and tripped over a guy rope.

"Ouch," he groaned.

In the evening Dad showed them how to use the stove safely. Then Dad said goodnight, and went indoors.

It was time to get the supper ready. Max pricked the sausages with a fork. Benny began to open the big tin of beans.

"Oooow!" cried Benny. He had cut his thumb on the sharp edge of the tin. Blood began to drip on to the grass.

“Don’t cry, Benny,” said Tom, putting on a plaster. “Otherwise you’ll have to go in.” Benny blinked back his tears.

They cooked the sausages and fried some eggs. The sausages were burnt quite black, and Benny gave most of his share to Tigger the cat. He tried not to think about the delicious shepherd's pie Dad had prepared for himself and Becky.

After supper Benny crawled into the tent and snuggled down in his duvet. A light drizzle had begun to fall and it felt very snug to be in a tent. Benny closed his eyes. He was very tired, for it was well past his bed-time.

The three big boys put their heads in at the tent.

"You can't go to bed *yet!*" they laughed. "Come and play football!"

Benny struggled out of the cosy tent to play football.

It was still raining a bit and Benny slipped in a patch of mud. Only when it was too dark to see the ball did the campers come back to the tent.

Tom and his friends began to play cards by torchlight. Benny shut his eyes and tried to get to sleep.

"We'll wake you for the midnight feast," said Max.

Benny was deeply asleep and dreaming he was back in his own bed when he felt someone shaking his shoulder.

"Wake up Benny! We've got the midnight feast ready!"

There were meat pies, jam sandwiches, sardines and a jug of custard.

"Don't want any," said Benny. "Just let me sleep!" He thought longingly of his little bed indoors.

The others munched the midnight feast noisily. Then they settled down and soon their snores filled the tent.

But now Benny was wide-awake.

His clothes felt uncomfortably damp. And he was sure a spider was crawling up his neck –

Benny decided to go home. Quietly he unzipped the tent.

Outside it was dark and spooky. The house looked very far away. An owl hooted . . . And just then Benny saw a small dark shape hurrying over the grass towards him. Could it be a RAT? He felt very scared. He'd heard that rats nibbled your toes!

Benny tumbled back inside the tent. He decided not to go back to the house after all.

He lay down again. He must get some sleep . . . But suddenly a great big SOMETHING jumped right on top of him!

But it was only Tigger the cat, come to visit the campers! Tigger curled up on the duvet. Benny was wet, he was cold, he was scared, but finally the sound of Tigger's purring sent him to sleep.

When he woke in the morning Benny felt stiff and aching all over. Sam was busy cooking on the little stove. But Benny didn't fancy any more burnt sausages or half-cooked eggs. He stumbled back to the house to join Dad and Becky for a proper breakfast.

That evening Benny could hardly keep his eyes open.

"Can I go to bed now, Dad?" he pleaded, straight after tea.

Dad came up to say goodnight.

"I've been thinking, Benjamin," said Dad. "Shall we all go on a camping holiday this summer?"

"Oh no!" said Benny. "Not CAMPING! I think, er, Becky is too young. She wouldn't enjoy it . . ."

And before Dad could turn out the light, Benny was fast asleep.